"...It was bedtime. He came from nowhere. I felt his snout on my neck--"

HE WAS OUT LIKE A LIGHT, SEZ WIFE

YouSnooze

"Piggie-Snoozing"--
Deep Sleep Follows Hog Attack

Authorities warn:
Be home by Bedtime!

PIG TALE:

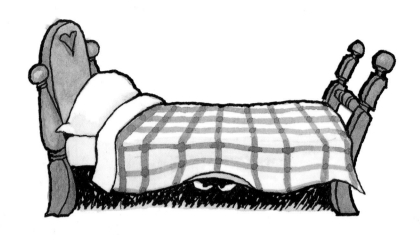

HE'S **HERE!**

HE'S **THERE!**

— **EVERYWHERE!**

And when **he finds you**,

SNORT · SNORT · Snort · SNORT · Sno

he'll snort you into a deep piggie snooze!

HEH-HEH, FANG YOU VERY MUCH!

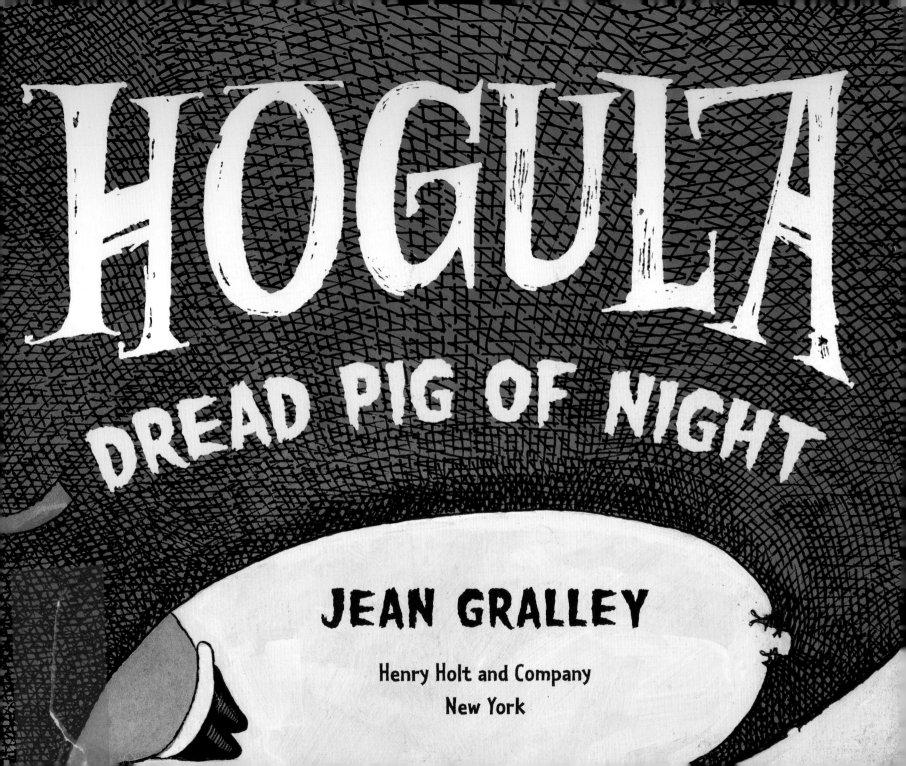

HOGULA

DREAD PIG OF NIGHT

JEAN GRALLEY

Henry Holt and Company

New York

For Paula Tohline Calhoun

Henry Holt and Company, Inc., *Publishers since 1866*
115 West 18th Street, New York, New York 10011

Henry Holt is a registered trademark of Henry Holt and Company, Inc.

Copyright © 1999 by Jean Gralley. All rights reserved.
Published in Canada by Fitzhenry & Whiteside Ltd.,
195 Allstate Parkway, Markham, Ontario L3R 4T8.

Library of Congress Cataloging-in-Publication Data
Gralley, Jean. Hogula, dread pig of night / by Jean Gralley.
Summary: Although he lives high on the hog in his castle on Grimy Pork Chop Hill, Hogula is
unhappy because he has no friends—until he meets Elvis Ann, Dread Queen of Kissyface.
[1. Pigs—Fiction. 2. Humorous stories.] I. Title. PZ7.G7653Ho 1999 [Fic]—dc21 98-36972

ISBN 0-8050-5700-5 / First Edition—1999
Printed in the United States of America on acid-free paper. ∞
The artist used gouache and ink on watercolor paper to create the illustrations for this book.

1 3 5 7 9 10 8 6 4 2

Hogula lived in a castle on Grimy Pork Chop Hill.

The castle was packed with mud and swill and old garbagey things, just the way Hogula liked it.

LOVELY.

Things were high on the hog on Grimy Pork Chop Hill.

But life was not complete.

Hogula had no friends. No friends to talk with. No friends to play with.
Except for his bats, no friends to hang with.

No friends at all.

Hogula very much wanted
to make a friend. But how?

Darkness fell, and Hogula departed for the Princes Mall that very night.

He liked it right away.

People liked him, too.

They liked his costume. They loved his fangs. And when he hung from the second-level balcony, they dropped their bags and cheered. And all those necks . . . oh my!

It was nearly bedtime, and Hogula's snorty snout itched to sink into them. He triple-flipped perfectly to the third-level balcony. Applause exploded below him.

No one noticed how tightly Hogula had to smile to keep from bursting into a snorty fit and snorting every neck in sight.

No one, except one shadowy figure who saw—and understood.

BING-BANG! BONG-BOING! The clock struck quarter to bedtime. The shoppers yawned and streamed out the double doors.

In no time at all, Hogula was alone.

He blinked.

He couldn't believe it. He'd shown off for an entire
evening and hadn't made a single, solitary friend.

Well, then!

His face burned pinker. His tail curled tighter.

No more Mr. Nice Hog! No more trying to make friends! Making friends was too hard!

From now on he would roam the world as the one, true thing he was:

THE AWFUL,

SNORTFUL,

FANGFUL AND FRIENDLESS

HOGULA,

DREAD PIG OF NIGHT.

This was Elvis Ann.

That night she went here, there, everywhere.

He was strange, he was wonderful, unlike anything she'd ever met before.
In some deep, mysterious way, Elvis Ann just knew they'd make a perfect team.
She wasn't sure about these other two.

Hogula smiled. Never had he wanted to snort a tempting bit of mortal so badly.

He moved to her face, past her face to her ear, and brought his twitching piggie snout to that delicious spot on her neck—when he noticed her lips were twitching, too!

Hogula paled. Before he could scream and jump out of the way—

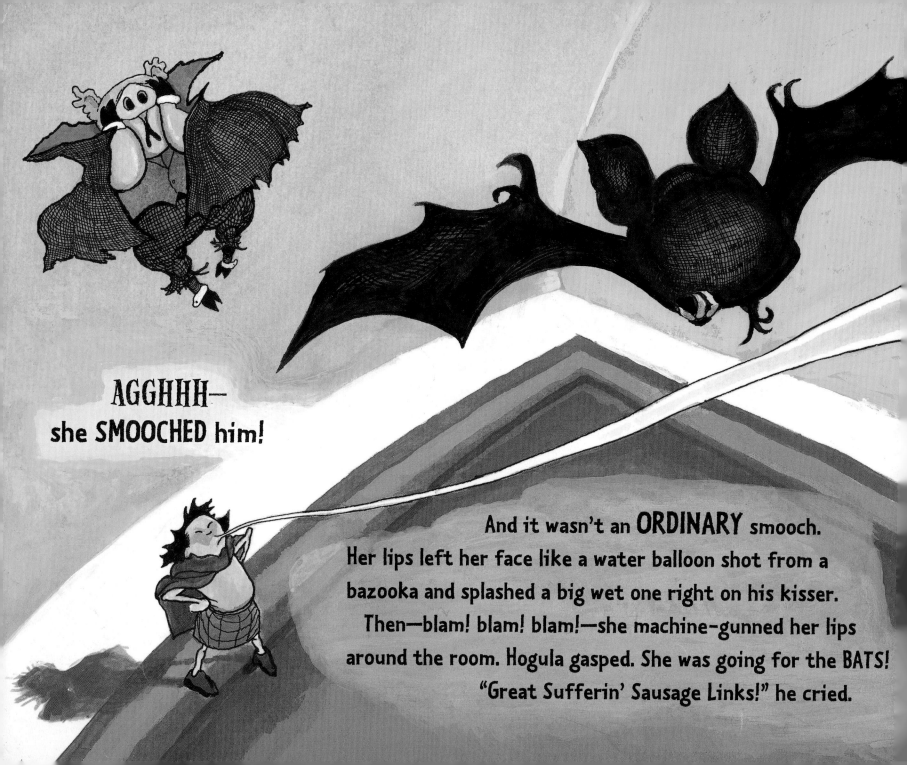

AGGHHH—
she SMOOCHED him!

And it wasn't an **ORDINARY** smooch.
Her lips left her face like a water balloon shot from a
bazooka and splashed a big wet one right on his kisser.
Then—blam! blam! blam!—she machine-gunned her lips
around the room. Hogula gasped. She was going for the BATS!
"Great Sufferin' Sausage Links!" he cried.

"I know who you are!"

Hogula was sure now. This was no ordinary mortal. This was *the* Elvis Ann, Dread Queen of Kissyface, known for kisses so slurpy and noisy and tickly and gross, even *he* was powerless before her fiendish charms.

Just as Elvis Ann had thought, they were a perfect match. There was no one in the world like Hogula, and no one like Elvis Ann. They were made-for-each-other friends.

To keep their friendship perfectly porky, they made three rules:

1) Hogula could snort.

2) Elvis Ann could kissyface.

3) They could not
snort or kissyface each other.

In friendship, sometimes you have to give a little to get a lot back.

To this very night, Hogula and Elvis Ann roam neighborhoods together, looking for those up past their bedtimes, deciding who to kissyface and who to snort and send into a deep, snoring, piggie-snoozie snooze.

THEY'RE **HERE!**

THEY'RE **THERE!**

THEY'RE EVERYWHERE!

And when they find you—

(kissy slurp!)
(snort snort!)

GOOD
BITE!!

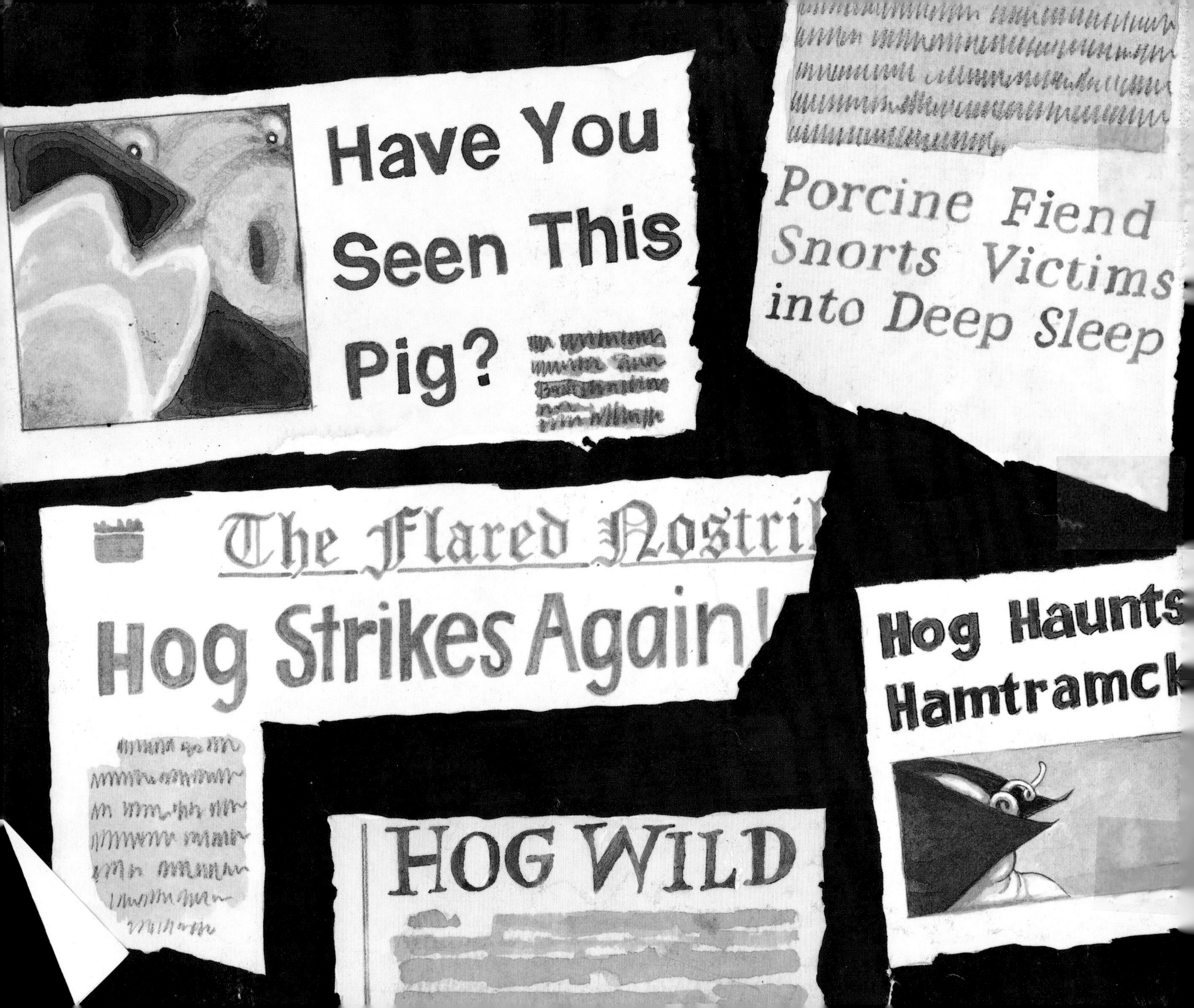
Have You Seen This Pig?
Porcine Fiend Snorts Victims into Deep Sleep
The Flared Nostril
Hog Strikes Again
Hog Haunts Hamtramck
HOG WILD